This book is a presentation of Atlas Editions, Inc. For information about Atlas Editions book clubs for children write to: **Atlas Editions, Inc.,** 4343 Equity Drive, Columbus, Ohio 43228.

Published by arrangement with Chronicle Books.
Weekly Reader is a federally registered trademark of Weekly Reader Corporation.

Printed in the USA

1998 edition

Library of Congress Cataloging-in-Publication Data

McGeorge, Constance W.
Boomer's big day / by Constance W. McGeorge; illustrated by Mary Whyte.
     p. cm.
Summary: Moving day proves confusing for Boomer, a golden retriever, until he at last explores his new home and finds his own favorite and familiar things.
ISBN 0-8118-0526-3 (hc)
[1. Golden retrievers—Fiction. 2. Dogs—Fiction. 3. Moving, Household—Fiction.] I. Whyte, Mary. II. Title.
PZ7.M478467Bo   1994
[E]—dc20   93-27273
                            CIP
                               AC

Weekly Reader Children's Book Club Presents

Boomer's Big Day

By Constance W. McGeorge
Illustrated by Mary Whyte

chronicle books

San Francisco

It was just after breakfast, and Boomer
was waiting to be taken for his daily walk
around the neighborhood.

But Boomer soon discovered this was not going to be an ordinary day. No one left the house after breakfast. No one would stop what they were doing to play with him. Everyone was very, very busy.

Boomer decided it was going to be one of those days when he had to play all by himself.

He searched the house for his favorite toy, an old green tennis ball. He looked in his toy basket—no ball. He looked under the sofa—no ball. He looked under all the beds in the house. But his ball was nowhere to be found.

Suddenly, the doorbell rang. Boomer barked and barked, but everyone told him to be quiet. Then strangers carrying large boxes came through the front door and into the house.

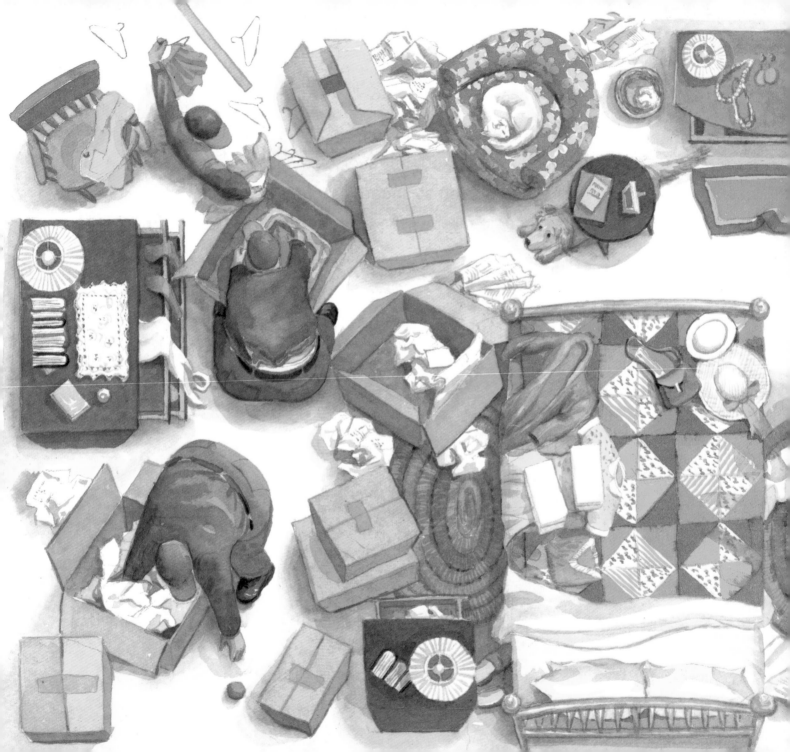

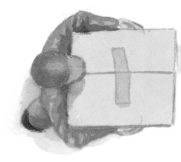

Soon there was activity everywhere. Boxes appeared in every room of the house. The strangers started pulling things out of closets, out of drawers, and out of cupboards.

Then they packed everything into boxes, and one by one, the boxes were carried out of the house.

Before Boomer knew it, the house was empty.

While the strangers loaded the boxes and furniture into a large truck parked in front of the house, Boomer's family loaded its van.

Finally, Boomer was led out of the house. He was told he was going for a ride. But lots of other things seemed to be going for a ride, too.

Boomer was very confused.

The ride was unlike any other Boomer had
ever taken. He could hardly see out the window.
Packages kept falling on him. The ride lasted a
very long time.

Finally, the van stopped in front of a house Boomer had never seen before. There were strange trees, strange flowers, and strange people passing by.

Boomer wondered where he was.

Boomer walked cautiously up to the front door of the house. He peeked in. The house was empty.

While the strangers unloaded the truck, and his family unloaded its van, Boomer went inside. He wandered from room to room. There was nothing to do and no one to play with.

Then Boomer discovered the backyard.

He couldn't believe his eyes!
There were things to sniff . . .

holes to dig . . .

squirrels to chase . . .

and best of all . . . there were new friends to be made!

At the end of the day, Boomer went inside.
Instead of being empty, the house was now full of
furniture and boxes.

Boomer found his dinner bowl in the kitchen.
His bed had been unpacked, too. And there,
beside it, was his old green tennis ball.

Boomer wagged his tail. Then, happy to be
home, he curled up and went to sleep.